50p

D1394687

Spencer's Spaghetti

Bill Gillham

Illustrated by Margaret Chamberlain

Methuen Children's Books

Spencer liked to eat
spaghetti.

But he liked playing
with it better.

He tied it into bows.

He lassooed the cat with it.

He even tried skipping
with it.

"Spencer! Stop playing
with your food!"

"Yes Mum," said Spencer.

He gave himself spaghetti
hair,

and frightened the dog.

"Spencer! Are you playing
with your food?"

"No Mum," said Spencer.

He made spaghetti flowers
on the table.

Then he made himself
spaghetti glasses.

The tomato sauce ran
down his nose.

It tasted better like that.

"Don't let me catch you playing with your food, Spencer!"

"No Mum," said Spencer.

What's Spencer making now?

A spaghetti hammock!

And when his Mum looked
round the door . . .

Spencer was fast asleep.

And what does this say
on the table?

How to pair read

1 Sit the child next to you, so that you can both see the book.

2 Tell the child you are *both* going to read the story *at the same time*. To begin with the child will be hesitant: adjust your speed so that you are reading almost simultaneously, *pointing to the words* as you go.

3 If the child makes a mistake, repeat the correct word but *keep going* so that fluency is maintained.

4 Gradually increase your speed once you and the child are reading together.

5 As the child becomes more confident, lower your voice and, progressively, try dropping out altogether.

6 If the child stumbles or gets stuck, give the correct word and continue 'pair-reading' to support fluency, dropping out again quite quickly.

7 Read the story *right through* once a day but not more than twice, so that it stays fresh.

8 After about 5–8 readings the child will usually be reading the book independently.

In its original form paired reading was first devised by Roger Morgan and Elizabeth Lyon, and described in a paper published in the Journal of Child Psychology and Psychiatry (1979).

First published in Great Britain in 1985
by Methuen Children's Books Ltd, 11 New Fetter Lane, London EC4P 4EE
Reprinted 1986
Text copyright © 1985 Bill Gillham. Illustrations copyright © 1985 Margaret Chamberlain
Printed in Great Britain ISBN 0 416 53030 3